BREAKING THE GLADIATOR

AN ALPHA ATTRACTION NOVELLA

NICOLA ROSE

Clare
It's Dark. It's Dirty.
Good luck looking me
in the eye again!!
Nicola Rose
x

For my favourite Motherfuckers!
Thanks for believing in me and giving me the push I needed!
(and the biscuits)

It is easier to find men who will volunteer to die, than to find those who are willing to endure pain with patience.

— Julius Caesar

1

CASSIAN

A champion gladiator doesn't feel love. How could he? His only passion is to win the next fight. Then the one after. And again.

If you're one of the lucky ones you might even get paid well for winning. You might be able to save the money for a different kind of future. It's rare, but there's a chance you could buy your freedom.

This is me. I'm that gladiator. I win all my fights and I care for nothing else.

But I have a problem, and right now she's riding my cock like I'm some sort of salvation. Like I offer *her* hope. As if I could offer anything to a woman like her.

I want to cut her out. Yank her from inside my chest, from that forbidden place that she creeps into. But my body sings under her devotion. It betrays my mind, making me forget. Coming alive at the touch of her fingers tracing the contours of my muscles. At the whisper of her lips as they brush against my ear. The pulse from her heart as it hammers against my own.

This is our time, when we can forget, when we can let

go. The voices in my head go quiet. No more shouting, no more blood, no more pain.

Her teeth catch my ear and I shudder. "Are you mine, now and forever?" she asks, stealing the breath from my lungs with a slow circling of her hips.

I palm her ass as she straddles me, making love so languidly, as if we really do have forever. "Always," I lie.

She leans down to taste my tongue. Casual. Erotic. Her little breasts offer the barest of caresses against my chest. "What if... if—" she starts, and stops, grabbing my roaming hands and going still. "Sssshh..."

I freeze, and listen for the terrifying sound of the ludus gates opening and closing with a gentle creak.

"Shit!" Livia lurches upwards, shoving me to my feet. "He's home."

"Felix? You said he was away for another two days?" I grab my leathers as she hastily throws on a tunic.

She smoothes the fabric over her slender curves and throws me a quick surveying glance. I'm just fastening a cuff to my forearm when she shouts, "Guard!"

Fuck!

He appears immediately, eyeing the cuff that is only half buckled. I drop my head and use every shred of willpower not to look upon her flushed face.

Noticing her undergarments by my feet, I subtly toe them under the bed, out of the way. I know what else she hides under there—

"Have Cassian taken back to the barracks immediately." Her voice has returned to that pompous one that makes my teeth grind. Domina of the house. All warmth vanished, like a breath of air on a cold day.

The guard takes my arms behind my back and leads me to the door.

"Cassian," she calls out, and we pause, my eyes resolutely on the ground where they belong. "Remember what I've told you at this meeting in preparation for the games tomorrow. It was imperative that I went over it with you in my husband's absence."

I don't need to see her face to know that she would be watching the guard as she spoke slowly, praying to the Gods that he would buy her story. Or at least play along. What she forgets is that just because they're beneath her, the slaves and guards aren't imbeciles. Everyone knows what's going on. And unless she develops a shred of kindness towards them soon, this will come crashing down around us.

"Domina," I mutter, dipping my head into a deeper nod, and the guard escorts me back to my cell.

2

LIVIA

I allow myself the briefest minute to calm my nerves and, hopefully, for the sin to wash away from my flushed skin. Then I go to find him. It isn't hard to locate his whereabouts within the ludus grounds. I only need to follow the giggles and yelps, the moans and grunts.

Entering the dining room on a gust of fake nonchalance, I find my husband thrusting himself down the mouth of his favourite slave girl, Aelia. Away for a week and he couldn't even be bothered to come and find me first. He barely acknowledges me as I approach, casting a disappointed glance up and down my body before alighting his sights on the three girls masturbating over our dining chairs. One of them has her naked ass on my own chair.

I force my shoulders back and take a deep breath. "Felix, my love. How were the meetings and sales?"

"Boring as a fuck with your wife on a rainy day," he replies, and Aelia giggles through her mouthful.

"You would allow her to disrespect me?" I swallow back the bitter taste in my throat.

"You disrespect yourself," he spits, never releasing the

hold on Aelia's head as he thrusts faster into her face. He grabs a piece of fruit from the table platter, takes a bite, and speaks again as he chews, "What happened to you? You don't sparkle like you used to."

"A jewel cannot shine without light," I mumble.

"What was that?"

I shove down every shred of dignity and slowly peel the dress from my skin, trying my hardest not to look into the corner of the room where I know his personal guard is standing. Titus has observed so many of my humiliations that it burns to even look at him now, knowing how much he loves it, knowing how much he surely wishes it was him dealing the damage. Something dark lurks in him. So dark that even Cassian sometimes comments on it; to warn me not to aggravate the guard, and never to find myself alone with him.

Felix quirks his brow as my tunic falls to the floor and reveals my lack of undergarments – as much a surprise to myself as it is to him. Stepping away from the fabric, I seat myself in his chair and spread my legs. Reluctantly, I tease my clitoris, but I don't feel anything. No sparks, no pleasure. I want to close my eyes, so I can better see Cassian behind my lids. Instead I keep my gaze fixed on my despicable husband and allow only the barest of thoughts to drift to my gladiator.

I feel his heavily tattooed hands on me; strong, yet gentle. I hear his voice in my ear; rough, like the crunch of stone underfoot—

"Livia," Felix barks, and my eyes snap open. It appears they had closed regardless. "Get over here. You look like you're having too much fun."

Heaven forbid.

I dutifully present myself to my husband, wincing as his eyes rake over me in their menacing way.

"Turn around," he orders, bending me over the dining table so that I have no choice but to face Titus. He will only fuck me like this now – from behind, so that he doesn't have to look upon my face. The face that will forever be scarred after a drunken fight and the slash of a broken bottle.

"You! Come here." Felix has discarded Aelia, leaving her on her knees. Even his favourite girl doesn't get decent treatment. He clicks his fingers to one of the others. "Stand before me girl. Let me see those perky young tits as I fuck this haggard old witch."

3

LIVIA

By the time Felix has satisfied himself by climaxing into every orifice of every girl present, the sun has crept over the horizon to a new day. I'm so tired, so desperate to curl up and relish the nothingness that only sleep can bring.

But today is the day of an important games on the calendar. There will be feasting, parades, animal displays, executions of criminals, and of course, the gladiatorial combats. And as the wife of such a high-class noble, I shall be expected to endure it all with a smile. Not only to endure, but to enjoy it. And I would, were I not so lost in fear.

Fear of being caught. Fear of losing him. Fear that one day he may die and I shall never feel that touch again.

"For the sake of Neptune's Cock, woman! Go bathe and change. You look like something I shit out after breakfast," Felix slaps my ass in dismissal.

So I follow his command, as if I'm no more than a slave myself. I clean, and dress, and after a long confused search find my undergarments under the bed – along with the kitchen knife that I keep there for safety.

All too soon I'm seated beside my husband in our front row tier at the arena, sweating in the blistering heat.

The parades pass in a blur, as do most of the attractions. I nod, and smile, and clap.

Felix talks business with a variety of men who come and go. Sometimes their wives join me and I have to make pleasant talk with them. I find one lady staring at my wrist and after that I remember to keep it hidden beneath the folds of my dress. Hiding the bruising from Felix's grip last night. At least today my eyes aren't black.

"He's going to make me a fortune, you know."

"Hmm?" Felix is staring and I realise he's speaking to me for the first time in hours. I have no idea how much of it I missed, but he looks irritated.

"Forgive me, who are we talking about?" I enquire.

"Cassian! For fuck's sake, woman, listen when you're spoken to."

I nod in apology. Titus, who is glued to Felix as always, offers me a sneer.

"It's imperative that we keep him well treated. Let the other gladiators witness the special treatment for a house champion, give them something to strive for. The lanista is training him hard, and in return he will be well fed and cared for. You will ensure this happens when I'm away on business," Felix continues, and I fear the flush that has surely crept into my cheeks. "Oh, and I already agreed with Vitus that for every fight he wins from here forward, he shall be rewarded with a slave girl for the night. He is a beast of a man and needs fulfilment."

I clear my throat, "As you wish."

4

CASSIAN

The underground chambers are stifling while we wait, already having been briefed and instructed on what's expected of us for this event. Some men are shackled, here only to be executed. No honour, no chance to fight. These men shrink into themselves, detaching from the horror that awaits.

Others, slaves like myself, pace anxiously, adjusting armour and weapons. Eager to get on with it. I stand still and quiet, though – watching them all. Assessing my opponents.

If we're contained in this tunnel for much longer, barely any air to breathe, then fights will break out before we even reach the arena.

The guards know it. The lanista knows it. They keep a hand on their weapons, ready to beat us back into submission if we unleash our fury too soon. Tensions are high. Death is expected and anticipated.

The only death I anticipate is that of my opponents. May the Gods have mercy on them, because I won't.

From the day I was taken as a teenage boy I've had to

bow down. To men, women, even children. I've been sold and beaten. Destroyed. Broken.

And then the pieces rebuilt into what they wanted. A monster. A *pet* monster. One who is strong enough to destroy them in a second, yet still bows down when asked.

In the arena I'm free. There, I bow to no one. There... they quiver before me and beg for mercy.

I'm loved. Adored. The crowd cheer and chant my name, because I'm someone.

I am Death.

5

LIVIA

The executions are boring. Once, I would have found them a thrill. Now they barely register through the haze in my brain. It's a struggle to focus on anything other than thoughts of him. Exhilaration and fear, bringing me to life.

But out here, enduring life as this woman; this fake, obedient wife? Here I feel nothing. The blood coating the arena does nothing to stir me, except perhaps to make me think more of him. To anticipate the beauty of the champion unleashed.

I'm restless, impatient for his turn. Felix can tell. He's giving me aggravated glares. I clutch my hands in my lap and watch the final parade streaming into the open space before us. The musicians and performers whip the crowd into a frenzy. They can't wait to see their favourite gladiator either. His popularity has tripled his value in recent months.

And there he is. The prized Thracian. A towering wall of solid muscle. Heavy black tattoos cover his arms, his entire back, right up his neck to his chin. Tattoos are considered a thing of punishment and shame. He has, of course, been branded with our house mark, but it is tiny compared to those that he has willingly applied. Money earned from his victories in battle has paid for them all, and he wears them with pride. He wants the world to know he is Thracian. Felix allows it because the crowd are mad for it.

Crazy for this true Barbarian brute. Savage and brutal. Exotic and exciting.

He stalks through the Gate of Life and takes his place in the centre of the arena, relishing in the frantic applause and cheering. The procession fades away, leaving only Cassian and his opponent – facing each other, awaiting the order to begin.

Cassian shrugs his shoulders, loosening muscles, and makes a final adjustment to the armour that covers one shoulder. Sword and shield loose in his confident hands. He toes the sand, not a care in the world, and then his head raises, his eyes scan the maddening crowd… and they settle on me.

An involuntary gasp escapes my throat. *What is he thinking?!*

But his gaze only lingers for a second, and then he's staring his opponent down. No one seems to have noticed the heat in my face, the panic in my eyes.

All except Felix's brother, Marcus, who smirks at me.

And then the fight has begun, and the deafening applause of the crowd is almost enough to drown out the hammering of my heart.

6

CASSIAN

I don't understand why, but I can't resist looking to her for approval. Or to check she's still there. Check that she's alright—

The Gaul's sword clangs down against the metal armour over my shoulder.

Fuck!

The impact brings me to my knees. There's blood. His sword probably scraped below the armour as he withdrew. I roll away as he comes in for another strike, and I'm swiftly on my feet again.

Did Felix see that I was looking at her? I should know better than to look. If he knew, if he found out—

The Gaul strikes again and I stumble, only just missing the blade. The crowd jeer in disapproval.

Fucking Gods! What is wrong with me?

I shake my head and snap my attention to my opponent. He's smaller than me, and slower. Far less skilled. The fact that he got a strike through on me is humiliating and the crowd know it.

Gathering the battle rage, honing it deep within my core,

I let silence wash through me. I can't hear the audience anymore. I track his movements as he goes to attack again, leaving it to the last second before I weave away. He turns, and I feint left, then strike on the right. My scimitar cuts across his thigh and blood spills to the sand.

Play with him. Gain favour back from the people...

Before he can compose himself I lunge, and deftly swipe across his abdomen, holding back enough that it will leave a nasty gash, but not enough to kill him. Not yet.

He roars in frustration and we clash together. Swords against shields, striking and blocking, a perfect dance of destruction. Better. Domina will approve. I can almost hear her cheers.

What if Felix was suspicious when he returned last night? What if I hadn't retreated quickly enough from their room, what if one of the guards had spoken out? He might have hurt her—

His sword swipes so close to my face that I hear the whoosh as it arcs through the air. My foot catches on something in the sand... he's on me again and he rams into my shoulder, the force slamming me to the ground.

I'm winded, looking up as he lifts his sword to plunge into my chest. This is it. All my years in this arena and I'm going to die at the hands of a weaker man. All I can hear are her cries. I pray they're only in my head and not out loud for all to notice. Will she mourn me?

Time has frozen. His sword is seconds from destroying me. Maybe I should allow it. Why do I even carry on with this existence?

Then I hear her voice. The gentle one that she uses only for me, only when I earn it.

As his blade begins its descent I lift a foot to his groin and catch him off guard. Within a moment I regain my feet and tackle him into a headlock. It's risky getting so close, but I grip with all my might until he has to drop his sword in an attempt to remove my strangling hold from his throat.

I glance up for approval from Felix. But I don't see him, I just see Marcus reaching across and twirling a lock of her flame red hair around his finger. Her bastard husband doesn't even notice, or care.

But I do. The sweep of rage through my core is so violent that I kick him away and splatter the Gaul's head, dragging my blade through his skull.

The crowd go silent for a heartbeat.

I didn't wait for Felix's nod of approval to deliver the killing blow. I don't care. My humiliation from this terrible fight is so deep; I would take any punishment rather than wait another second to end the Gaul.

He nearly beat me.

Fuck the Gods!

This woman will be the death of me. Soon, I will die on these sands, and it won't be with honour, it will be with shame.

7

LIVIA

"What in Jupiter's fucking name was that?" Felix fumes, flinging the door mercilessly on its hinges as we enter the villa, Titus following behind. Bodyguard, and all-round overconfident bastard.

He doesn't want me to try and answer his question. I'm not qualified to have an opinion on these matters. He just wants to shout and vent, and when he's finished yelling at me he'll do the same at Vitus, our lanista, responsible for training Cassian. For training all eight of our gladiators.

Felix spins on his heels to face me, purple with rage.

"He did win, though," I offer.

"Barely! He was like a fucking newly-birthed lamb out there. All over the place. I've never known him to be so distracted in the arena. I will not tolerate this underperformance."

I'm grateful at the tentative knock on the door, and by the sight of Vitus as he enters meekly. Good. Please, Gods, let him take the brunt of the punishment.

I will deal with Cassian's punishment myself. The thought brings a tingling ache between my legs. Yearning. Need.

I clear my throat.

"And to think just earlier today I was talking of showering him with women and luxuries!" Felix bellows in Vitus's face.

Respect for Vitus, he doesn't shy away. But then he wouldn't. None of the gladiators would. Yes, they will nod and bow and show respect. But they won't show weakness. Vitus was a fine fighter in the arena in his time. His victories earned him the coin and respect to buy his freedom and become a trainer.

"With all due respect, Dominus, I feel you must still reward him for the victory," Vitus speaks softly. Soothing a temper-prone child. "A win is a win, and if you back down on promised rewards now then it will dampen morale of the whole ludus."

Titus flexes his fingers, trying to intimidate the lanista, but steps back when Felix nods in agreement. "Fine. He will have his woman and his feast, but first he will be punished. Let him experience both and choose for himself which post-games activities he would prefer to receive from here on."

"A sound strategy," Vitus bobs his head, as if 'Felix the Genius' had thought of it himself.

Felix eyes him sceptically. "Reduce his general leisure time and increase his training. I expect results at the next games, Vitus, or your rank will be removed. And ensure that his punishment is severe."

"Of course, Dominus."

A sick thrill runs up my spine in anticipation. Today could have got him killed. That's my fault. I've shown him too much affection and he lost his focus. I won't make that mistake again.

8

LIVIA

I'm standing in the middle of an arena, covered in the blood of all those who have hurt me over the years. I lift my arms in victory and spot Cassian stalking towards me. I run to him—

But then I'm back home. At the place I grew up. Images of Cassian are ripped from me and leave an empty, gaping hole—

I'm behind the old villa, where my father keeps the wild dogs. They pace restlessly, back and forth, up and down in their small cage. I inch closer to the bars, daring myself to get near to them. They're the size of wolves. The alpha prowls closest to the bars, sizing me up.

He's the biggest, but even he has bones protruding from his skin. Not enough food. Never enough to make them happy. That way, when they are released in the arena, they will turn on whatever is put before them. Sometimes, they even turn on each other within this cage. They'll pick off one of the smaller ones and feast on it.

Right now they just look sad. Whimpering. Hungry. Pacing.

They fascinate me. I come and sit here every day to watch them. Mesmerised by their raw power. Marvelling at how they can turn from feral wolf one minute, to whimpering hounds the next.

The alpha always watches me with his calculating eyes. He's intelligent. Today, something feels different when he stops to observe me. His eyes almost seem human. I'm sure he's trying to tell me something. Like he trusts me. My friend. Perhaps we have bonded from all the time watching each other.

It doesn't feel right. These creatures should not be caged like this. He's beautiful. He should be free.

I reach a finger to his nose and let him sniff. He doesn't growl. He doesn't shy away. He just holds his ground and keeps staring at me. I want to hold him, soothe him.

Without thinking, I release the door on the cage and set them loose. Most of them flee in a frenzied rush, but the alpha – he runs directly through the open door of our villa and the screaming begins.

First my mother, then, briefly, my baby sister.

Then it's just my mother. Screaming and screaming and screaming.

9

LIVIA

I wake from the dream drenched in sweat. But it's not just a dream. It's a memory.

So many nights it comes back to me. A clear recounting of the events that happened when I was just twelve years old.

Grabbing a drink of water, I slump back against the soaked bed sheets, and trace a finger over a scar on my arm. One of many that decorate my body. The punishments I received from not only my father, but also my mother, were brutal. As if I was no more than a slave myself. Whipped and beaten and degraded.

I can still hear my father's voice, haunting me daily.

They are beasts, Livia. Break them down. Tear them apart. Then build them up, and you will own them. But never forget what they're capable of.

He wasn't just talking about the dogs. Slaves, gladiators, hounds... it was all the same.

My parents never recovered from the grief of that beast mauling my baby sister to death. None of us did. My father found the most comfort in alcohol. Eventually he lost everything, every last coin. Thankfully I was already married to Felix by then. But it took a lot of work on my part to stop Felix from kicking me out once he realised my family had nothing. Once he knew that I was penniless and numb.

I had never told him what happened with my sister, but my father made certain to, in his rage at losing everything. His final push to try and hurt me. I think Felix actually smiled after hearing that story. It clicked into place and he realised just how damaged I was. Just how much he would be able to use me and abuse me, and that I would not retaliate.

Because I'm worthless. Nothing.

The screams are still ringing in my ears.

I deserve nothing.

I shake away the memories and force myself from the bed.

Mercifully, Felix left our home again last night for another 'business trip'. He knows when I have the dream, when I wake screaming, and he often smiles cruelly, ready to break me apart further. But today he is gone and I sigh in relief. I don't know what he's really doing, and I don't care. He's away, and that is a blessing.

And what do I do with this free time? Do I socialise with friends? Take a walk into the city? Go shopping?

No. I spend an hour listening to the crack of a whip against Cassian's back. The noise drifts all the way from the barracks, across the training ground, and through to my room. Never a groan or a cry, though. He takes the beating in silence.

I strain to hear more. To hear just one groan of pain.

The pressure building between my thighs is unbearable. I pace anxiously up and down, changing my mind over and over about what I should do.

I should go.

No. I should stay.

But I must go. I have to go.

I can't go. It's getting too risky.

And then my personal maid arrives to wash my hair, and before I know it the words have already slipped out, "I believe Vitus is nearly finished with Cassian. He'll be tired and agitated. You should go to him, he could probably use your touch right now..."

Alba startles as if I've struck her down. No doubt terrified that I am indeed about to do so, for knowing of the secret relationship she has with the lanista. "Your secret is safe, Alba. Go to him. Consider it a reward for your loyal service."

Confusion pulls at her delicate features.

So maybe niceness to slaves isn't generally my approach. They must be kept in line. But Cassian has told me repeatedly that they won't keep our secrets unless I start offering them something in return. How hard can it be?

"Go," I say, a little too harshly.

I watch her scurry away like a startled mouse and force myself to count to one hundred before I walk as casually as I can, through the barracks, directly towards the punishment room.

10

LIVIA

Every gladiator immediately stops what they're doing and stands to attention as I pass through, the fabric of my floor length dress sweeping along the dusty floor with a gentle hiss. The smell of sweat and dirt has my heart racing. That intoxicating aroma of masculinity. This is where the beasts dwell, and my heart skitters in approval.

I reach my destination and all is quiet from within. The guard on duty doesn't know where to look as I come to halt. I didn't see Vitus on my way through, and I could guarantee that if he was anywhere in the vicinity when the lady of the house entered his barracks, then he'd have been stood to attention. Which meant Alba hadn't failed me. I suppressed a smile at the thought of their fumbling fucking somewhere on the grounds, hidden and dangerous.

"I need to speak with Cassian about the next games. There are details my husband forgot to pass on. Ensure we are not disturbed," I motion for the guard to open the door with a dismissive wave.

"But, Domina, should the lanista not be present?"

I give him a look that could melt lead. "You question the

orders of your Dominus? I am to deliver this information right now, and since the lanista appears to be absent, perhaps I will have to report his own failings—"

"No... no, it's just... Cassian is in no fit state. I will have him cleaned and dressed and brought to your room. This isn't the place for a lady..."

"I don't have all evening to be dealing with my husband's tedious work! I will do this right now and then get out of this festering shit-pit."

"As you wish, Domina." He reluctantly opens the door and my legs turn to jelly at the sight of Cassian – naked, chained with his hands strapped high above his head, bloodied and beaten.

11

CASSIAN

A woman's bare feet stop before me, just visible beneath the fabric of her flowing dress. She doesn't speak. Doesn't move. Just stands there – tauntingly close.

I don't have the energy to lift my head and look at her. But I wouldn't do it, even if I did. I'm not that stupid. There's only one reason she's here, and it's not to comfort me.

Muscles tear in my shoulders from the way I'm dangling in chains. I could have been here for minutes, or hours... when you're in so much pain time loses meaning.

But she's about to bring a whole other type of agony.

Beautiful and deadly.

She will break me apart from the inside out.

I will hate her.

But I will love her.

And I will pray to the Gods that I can just die to end this sweet torture.

12

LIVIA

"Be grateful Felix hasn't ordered harsher punishments for you, Cassian. You could be facing far worse right now if your lanista hadn't spoken for you." My voice is rasping. Breathy. Excitement tickles my skin.

"Gratitude, Domina," he says, deep and low.

His head hangs forward, eyes always to my feet. Tattooed muscles bulge from his enormous biceps, his broad chest pulled tight with the strain from being bound in such a way, crushing air from his lungs. Hands tied high up overhead, his toes barely able to touch the ground.

His body is a patchwork of brutality. I move slowly around him, assessing the damage. The face that is bruised and cut, the black and blue ribs. Round to the welts that criss-cross his back. The whip lays discarded in a corner.

Some of the injuries were obtained in the arena, but many of them are at the lanista's own hands. I wouldn't be surprised if he'd even instructed the other gladiators to tear some strips from their champion's flesh.

I touch my fingertips to the nape of his neck and glide

them slowly down his spine. He hisses on a deep intake of breath.

Leaning in close, I nuzzle my lips to his ear lobe. "You're a fool for allowing yourself to become so distracted in the arena," I whisper against his neck. "If you ever look upon me again in public I will see to it that you don't walk for weeks. Do you understand?"

"Yes, Domina."

"It was downright idiocy." I move to the corner and take hold of the whip, gliding it through my hands. "Do you not realise the delicate line we tread here? If Felix were to find out..."

I pause, allowing his head to sag forward further, and then I lash out — the whip striking true and firm across his lower back. His head jolts up, but he doesn't make a sound.

I lash harder... once, twice, and still he's mute. But every muscle in his body is rigid. His arms tremble against their restraints. My barbarian. Capable of killing any man with his bare hands, trembling at my touch.

"Do you wish me to rub salt into these wounds?" I ask, prodding the end of the whip against an angry red mark.

"No, Domina," he replies through clenched teeth.

"Then let me hear your pain, gladiator."

Break them down.

I strike again and again. His answering groan increases with every crack. He will never cry out for me, never yell. But he will groan, and wetness pools between my thighs in response.

Dropping the whip, I move to his front, trailing my hand lazily around his waist. He shudders, but his glorious member hangs flaccid. I trace the solid muscles in his abdomen, up and over his chest, pausing to circle his nipples.

Following the touch with my mouth, I plant kisses over every bit of his bloodied and dirty chest. He's sweaty, dusty, beaten. But never broken. No matter how I try.

The tang of his blood on my tongue is sinful. I lap it up, chasing a solitary trickle from his chin, up his cheek and to its source above his eyebrow.

He comes to life and I feel his unwavering erection press against me. Pushing forward, I grind into his shaft until he can't help the soft moan that escapes. That moan has me dropping to my knees and worshipping his cock.

I glide my tongue along the tip, circling round and down, licking all the way to his balls. Gripping the base with a firm hand, I pump softly, licking and sucking at only the head. His hips struggle to push forward, to drive himself further into me, but he barely has the balance.

I draw back. *Make him wait. Make him suffer. Break him down.*

When he stops pushing forward I return my mouth to his tip and continue to tease. I take my time, knowing that Vitus could return at any moment, the danger edging me on. One hand moves round to his ass and his balls tighten. He knows what's coming. Or at least, he thinks he does, but there's no way this would be enough punishment for the threat he posed to us in that arena.

I haven't even started.

I stop, just before he reaches climax, and then I start again.

Repeat. Over and over until his growls can probably be heard the other side of Rome.

Taunting the beast while he's chained... it's low. And the power surging through my veins is beautiful. I'm flying. Soaring. The desperate need between my legs is torture to myself, but I carry on regardless, letting his rage build.

“Look at me,” I command; knowing full well that to do so breaks every rule he’s had beaten into him over the years. His head remains bowed, teeth clenched in fury.

“Now!” I yell, before sucking him deep into my throat on a greedy slurp.

His eyes snap to mine and I nearly choke on the mouthful. So much hatred. So much unbridled anger in those mesmerising blue eyes. It’s all there. All the bloodlust, all the desire and death. Staring right through me.

I move a hand between my thighs and rub at myself while he watches me suck him.

“Please,” he groans. “Domina, please, I can’t...”

He tightens, the release about to break through.

And I step away.

His roar echoes through my very bones. I will fill up on his hatred, devour his wrath. The next time he’s brought to my room he’ll unleash the beast upon me and I will ride the waves of his pain.

I straighten out my robes and move in closer, my lips a whisper from his. Not touching, not giving in to the soaring arousal that has my core twisting in frustration. “A slave girl will be brought to you tonight, as reward for your abysmal victory in the arena.”

His eyes widen in horror. “No, you can’t. Don’t make me do that. I can’t—”

“You can, and you will.”

Panic threatens to engulf those shimmering eyes. He can face death on the battlefield with zero emotion, but this...

“Please, Domina.” I’ve never heard him beg with such conviction.

“If you don’t, it will raise further suspicions. You are a gladiator and you will fuck her like one.”

“You know what will happen—”

"Yes, I do. And if I think you have held back you'll be punished further. You will set free that fucked-up head of yours and you will rain down your fury upon her."

"I don't want any other. I only need you."

"Which is why you will take her. Consider this your final punishment, and if you ever look at me from the arena floor again, I will not hesitate to destroy you."

13

LIVIA

Sagging against the wall, I'm back in my room, gasping for breath between the tears.

I have to do this.

Do not show weakness. Break them...

If we're caught because of his recklessness then Felix will ensure we both suffer for an age. Then he'll end our misery in death.

I think, sometimes, Cassian sees me as his saviour. I'm everything – his world. He hates me and loves me all at the same time. He can't forgive me for the way he's treated, for the things we've put him through. But he wants to. He wants to push past that pain and love me. Or maybe he's just using me too. Does he just want to be free? Does he think I can set him free?

He's wrong. I cannot. And why would I? I've learned my lesson about releasing beasts. He's no different to that alpha dog. If I let him off the leash he'll turn around to bite me. Besides, I like the power I have over him. I like that he'll bend to my will and bow before me... and in the next moment claim me like a crazed animal. I'm his owner, and his prey… I'm *everything*.

I take deep breaths and bury the anxiety. Swiping away tears and swallowing down the sympathy, losing it amongst the grime in my rotten core.

I will not show weakness.

Torturing myself brings a kind of pain that I like. One that I'm in control of. I choose how much it hurts. I choose when it happens and how much I will tolerate. Because this is all I'm worthy of. Pain and loss. Heartache. I don't deserve anything more, so I become evil and transfer my suffering to someone else.

I want him to hurt as much as I do. And then, when he can bear no more, I want him to hurt me right back. To use me and abuse me. I want the monster – all of him.

He loves me. He would never really hurt me, not in any way that I didn't ask for.

Felix hurts me for nothing but his own pleasure, all the love we once shared has died. His slave girls bring him more satisfaction than I do. I'm nothing but a money-grabbing whore. Here to look pretty on his arm and attend his needs behind closed doors.

But Cassian? The way he hurts me speaks to the darkest part of my soul.

And the darkness answers.

14

CASSIAN

I'm finally released from the shackles and left to clean myself up. Every movement should be agony, but I can hardly feel it. The welts on my back need medical attention though, or they'll become infected.

My performance in the arena was inexcusable. Allowing myself to be distracted by a woman was pure weakness, and I should have died out there on that sand. I didn't deserve to win.

No Thracian warrior worth anything would feel the way I do. I bring shame to my kind.

Having such feelings towards her… unforgiveable. Pathetic.

How can someone who relishes their control in such a way be anything but a vile stain on us all?

I hate her. She's the embodiment of everything I loathe.

So why does a lead weight sit in my chest when we're apart? Why do I care about the bruises she bears from other men? It's no worse than she dishes out to everyone around her.

She *deserves* pain and suffering. She can't even begin to understand what life is like for those beneath her...

If only her eyes wouldn't soften when she lets her guard down.

If only I didn't notice the way she trembles when her husband is near.

If only I didn't know that there was goodness hiding inside her, just waiting to be set free.

15

LIVIA

The anticipation of the thrill, and the heartache, that I'm about to endure is almost too much to bear. I've been careful not to send him his woman until long after nightfall, and the wait is agonising.

Finally, when it's the right time, I creep through the barracks, past all the sleeping gladiators. Vitus is secreted away in his private chamber with his love. A couple of guards remain on watch, but they don't dare to utter a word as I pass them.

Reckless. I'm getting just as reckless as he. Every time I move past a guard I know I'm courting with death. If one of them were to dare speak out against me...

I pull up sharply at Cassian's cell, and peer through the bars into the darkness. A single candle is lit, casting him in an eerie low light. Of course he heard me coming. Was no doubt waiting for it. His shoulders slump as I lean against the bars.

The girl is seated next to him on the bed. Beautiful little Aelia.

Felix only instructed that Cassian should be rewarded

with a girl, he didn't specify which one. He'll be furious when he finds out that I sent his favourite plaything to the beast. But I'll take his punishment, it will be worth it.

I smile sweetly at Aelia and she grimaces. In her fluster from the gladiator next to her she's forgotten to fear me, and looks directly into my eyes. Good. I shall enjoy this so much more if she looks to me in despair. It might erase the sound of her patronising giggles in my head.

"Were you waiting for me to get started, or..." I trail off, eyebrows raised at Cassian.

"Please," he tries one more time. "Is it not enough that I bleed for you in the arena? You must bleed my heart dry, too?"

"Do not make me have to instruct you again."

Slowly, so slowly, he stands. Resigned.

His venom has him staring me down, too. He looks right through my soul with a mixture of pleading and exhilaration. Wildness. He drops the flimsy leather covering from his manhood and he's already hard, despite himself. Good boy.

Aelia obliges and removes her tunic. She shyly spreads her legs, as if she doesn't spread them every day for whichever man demands it. Just like we all do...

Cassian doesn't bother with any kissing or touching. He simply presses himself to her opening and enters on a gentle push. Drawing back, fully out, he follows with another, and another. Slowly, calmly. As if he were making love to me.

She moans in delight and reaches out to touch him, but he grunts his disapproval and swats her away, pinning her hands over her head.

The candle flickers and shadows dance across the contours of his abdominals. Sculpted to perfection. He's cleaned away most of the blood, but his body is covered in wounds, both old and new. The body of a fighting champion. A man created to serve one purpose – to entertain. To awe and inspire, to repulse and to thrill.

His pace quickens. He's going to try and end this quickly before the beast has time to prowl from the shadows.

"Don't you dare," I warn, and he pauses, slowing his journey.

"Show me," I whisper, my hand already rubbing at the nub between my legs. "You're nothing. No one but a disgusting creature. Show me what I do to you."

His answering snarl has me plunging a finger up inside my wetness.

The dark, swirling tattoos on his back come alive with the rippling and flexing of muscle. And then they go still. His whole body rigid.

The darkness is waking up.

16

CASSIAN

The darkness inside stirs. The same evil that awakens in the arena.

Fucking and fighting are my only releases. These are the only moments I can let go, when I can be free. But they get muddled in my head. They're too connected. As soon as the adrenalin flows, the beast emerges.

It doesn't matter that sex should be calm and beautiful – the demons wake up and the fog settles, and I can't control myself.

She knows this. Livia knows that the only time in my life when I have laid with a woman and *not* experienced that rage – is when I have slept with her. Through all the hatred and pain she causes, she still has the power to take it away. When she's soft, and tender, and my body melts into hers... the darkness vanishes and I can make love.

She knows this... and that's why she sent Aelia to my cell tonight. To release the tortured soul that she prodded and pushed in the punishment room. To marvel and enjoy... to fucking *enjoy* watching him unleashed on another.

Aelia lets out a squeak of pleasure. Her furrow is so tight and hot. I try to slow down, but it's too late. I can't see anything but haze. Every part of me surges for the thrill, muscles locked with rigid tension, my balls aching for release.

I thrust so hard that her head slams into the wall. She squeals and I pound harder. Every whimper that falls from her lips makes me want more. Harder. Faster. I can't tell if it's awe or fear as she stares up at me like a lost rabbit. So tiny, so breakable.

She's screaming in pain and pleasure as I nearly split her in two with violent thrusts.

"Louder," Livia commands. "Let the whole ludus know what you filthy creatures are doing."

I let out a roar and Aelia's shriek is almost delirious.

Visions sweep through my mind, right behind my eyes. All I can see is violence and blood. All I can hear is the agony of death, and the crack of a whip. My body locks into fight or flight.

And I will always fight.

I dare to glance at Livia. I shouldn't have.

The sight of her, dripping with lust, eyes glazed with passion...

I hate her.

I fucking love her.

My hands tighten around Aelia's throat and her eyes bulge.

I don't take my eyes from my Domina.

Not when Aelia's cries quieten to a gargle.

Not when the gargle quiets to nothing.

Not when I shoot my seed so far into her that my chest explodes in ecstasy and sorrow.

No. I do not take my eyes from my Domina. Because

tomorrow I will have to stare at her feet and pretend this never happened.

So I glare at her now, and I etch the awe on her face into my memory. The next time she sees my cock, it won't be a slave girl getting choked to the point of passing out.

It will be her.

17

LIVIA

The next day I awake and set about the usual routine without a glimmer of hesitation. If I falter, I will fall.

The slaves are quiet. The girls hush as I pass them, and serve me breakfast with extra caution. I catch a glimpse of Aelia through the kitchen, trying to hide the deep purple bruising on her neck with a strip of fabric. She scurries away before I can contemplate giving her an order. Or an apology.

No. No apology. Never show weakness. They will turn on you.

I choose to eat breakfast on the balcony overlooking the courtyard, where Vitus is already up and training our men. Disappointingly, Cassian is nowhere to be seen.

They are truly works of art, these gladiators. They repulse and inspire in equal measure. Everyone loves to hate them. Women pretend to be offended, but they all want to fuck a gladiator. And any man is deluding himself if he pretends he doesn't wish to have that power for a moment; to stand in an arena and conquer another.

Beyond the courtyard, the gates open and for a second I

panic that Felix has returned early again. I'm not ready for the confrontation when he sees the state of his favourite girl.

But it's not Felix that meanders through the grounds with a lazy smile. It's his brother, Marcus.

My stomach drops through the floor. Worse. So much worse than Felix being home.

At least suffering at my husband's hands is to be expected. I can live with it. But when it's his brother? The shame already coats my tongue, which sticks in my dry throat.

Marcus glances up to the balcony and gives me a wink.

And Cassian stalks from the shadows, looking like he might burn the world to ashes.

18

CASSIAN

I can't hold back.

Marcus cannot be here. Not today. I'm not in the right state today...

I move toward him and Vitus grabs my arm. I almost whirl and rip out his throat, barely getting a grip of myself.

"Stand down, gladiator," Vitus warns.

It's too late. I can't...

The haze settles. I can't bear it. *Not today, not today...*

Marcus has disappeared into the house.

My fists clench at my sides. I strain against Vitus' hold. Every part of me draws toward the villa. I must protect her. I'm her gladiator. Her warrior. I cannot stand back...

"I said, *stand down*, Cassian," Vitus growls in my ear. "Take it out on Caius." He puts a blunt wooden sword into my hands and shoves me onto the training ground.

19

LIVIA

"Marcus, what a pleasant surprise," I breeze, pottering around my room, busying myself with cleaning, which we both know is the job of the slaves.

"Livia," he nods. "I trust you are managing your husband's affairs in his absence?"

"Of course. All is well."

"Wonderful. You won't mind if I carry out a little inspection, then? You know how he frets when he's away. I won't be long..."

"Certainly. Where would you like to begin?" My voice hitches on the last word as his eyes rake greedily over me.

"Oh, I think we'll begin right here, Livia," he smiles.

"I see. Of course."

I should try to fight it. I should scream, or run. But where would I go? Who would even help me?

I'm alone. And I will face it with my head held high.

Felix doesn't care. Why should anyone else?

And so I bite back the tears as he pushes me to my knees. I stop myself from screaming the insults that want to break free. I take his cock, in every hole that he sticks it. And I take the beating that goes with it.

20

LIVIA

When Marcus is finished with me we head to the courtyard so that he may observe the gladiators. We watch them spar, and while he's distracted I try to organise my ruffled hair, pulling it down over my face in a vain attempt at hiding the cut lip. Goodness knows what my eye looks like, but it's puffed up and I can barely see through it.

I can see enough, though, to know that Cassian is fighting as if he were in the arena and not the training ground. He growls and roars, and swings the wooden sword down on his opponent with such force that blood flies and stains his own chest. Vitus snarls and goes to whisper in Cassian's ear. His back straightens and my breath catches.

This could be very bad.

Marcus watches them intently and, after a few barked commands, he has Vitus lining the men up for inspection. I trail a pace behind as he walks along the line, looking down his nose at the lesser beings before him.

He pauses in front of Cassian and I think everyone stops breathing.

Cassian bristles. His eyes downcast, but the anger simmering in them.

A smile creeps across Marcus's face as he looks from Cassian, and back to me.

He can't know! He can't possibly know. Please...

"Vitus," he suddenly barks. "My brother left clear instructions that this gladiator be put on increased training and reduced rations until his performance improves."

"That is correct—" Vitus starts.

"He doesn't look like he's remorseful, or that he has paid anywhere near enough for his underperformance."

I look at Cassian's body, covered in welts and bruises, and want to scoff at the absurdity of that statement. I can feel how badly my gladiator wants to look at me, how much he wants to rip the very head clean off Marcus's shoulders.

Marcus turns to me once more, wickedness playing on his smile. "I thought you could keep control of this place in your husband's absence, Livia? Are you being soft on these beasts? Perhaps you need me to move in for a while—"

"No," I gasp, higher pitched than I'd have liked. Cassian's jaw is grinding so tightly his teeth may crumble to dust.

He can't know. Marcus must not be given any clue as to my weakness. We will all perish.

"You're right," I stammer. "Cassian is the vilest of them all. Only last night I had to stop him before he killed that poor slave girl. It's lucky I heard her cries and went, since the guards were sleeping." A flicker of disbelief passes over all their faces – Cassian, and the men, but they remain mute, and I continue, "If he wasn't bringing in so much money I'd suggest that Felix sells him. I can hardly stand to look at him."

I see Cassian's fists clench and unclench, trying so hard to calm himself. Vitus looks ready to step in.

Slowly, Cassian raises his head to look directly upon Marcus, and the world tips from beneath my feet.

21

CASSIAN

Don't look.

Don't look.

Every part of me screams with the instinct not to look at him.

But I can't stop myself. And when my eyes meet his – so smug and self-assured, I would give anything to gauge them out with a spike.

"I'm in good company. You know all about making girls cry, too, don't you Marcus?" I spit the words into his face and the gasps of everyone around are loud enough to knock a modicum of sense into me. I drop my head back down.

Too late.

Not only had I looked into his eyes uninvited, I'd even used his name.

Weighted silence follows the sharp intake of breath. Waiting.

We wait. The calm before the storm.

Vitus slams into me from behind, forcing me to my knees. Then he's in front, drawing his knee into my face. Blood rushes from my nose and drips to the dirt.

"Apologies, Master Atticus, I will deal with this immediately," Vitus grovels, his face turning whiter by the second.

"Yes, you will," Marcus storms. "This gladiator will not rest for two days. You keep him moving every minute of the day. And when he can't breathe and passes out, you wake him up and get him going again. Understood?"

"Of course."

"Felix will be hearing of this and you can bet your life that unless Cassian achieves something miraculous at the next games, then his miserable existence here on earth will come to an even more miserable end."

22

CASSIAN

Marcus left long ago. Not brave enough to try and discipline me himself. Perhaps he has some brains after all.

I'm still jogging around the yard, every step threatening to break me with exhaustion.

Livia has not moved from her seat beside the courtyard. She sits, and watches, lost and glazed over. There is nothing in her eyes. No warmth. No compassion.

Her beautiful face is bruised. She often tries to hide the scar on her cheek. Now she tries even harder to hide behind that fiery red hair, hanging limply over one side of her face.

She's ice. Cold and fracturing. Little cracks are blossoming through her shell. Soon, if she doesn't stop it, the cracks will spread and she'll fall apart.

Vitus has become distracted with a conversation and I slow my pace, hesitating by her chair as I pass.

"You're poisonous," I say on a sharp breath. "Your venom is so deep beneath my skin that I can't tell where the most pain comes from – the arena, or your mouth."

I don't linger long enough for her to reply, but I do note the shift in her eyes, from disconnected to burning fiercely.

23

LIVIA

It's my duty to ensure the slaves know their place. And to keep the people entertained when they are presented with my gladiators. I don't have much purpose in life, but that's one obligation I can't shy from. If I fail to keep control of my own house then I'll lose everything. I'll end up with even less than I have now. I can handle the emptiness in my soul, but not in my pocket. I can't become destitute.

Yet the haunted look in his eyes crucifies me. The hurt, anger, regret. I die a little more on the inside, but I'll never show it.

Sweeping from my chair, I catch up with Cassian on his lap of the courtyard. He slows to a walk as I step in pace beside him, ignoring the wary look from Vitus.

"Speaking out against Marcus was unforgiveable. You push your luck too far. Your ego swells with my attention and you forget your place," I hiss.

He'll get himself killed. I can't stop the punishments that Felix will inflict.

"Apologies, *Domina*," he spits my title with disgust, panting with exertion. "Next time, would you like me to bend over so he can shove his miniscule cock further into my anus? Maybe he'll shove it in so hard it'll come out my throat? Would you like that? Would you like to see him fuck me the way he fucks you? We both know how much you enjoy watching—"

I grab his shoulder and pull him to a stop. Then I slap him around the face. Hard.

"I did what I had to do, and I'd do it again. If I didn't, there would be no hierarchy, no order—"

He drags a finger slowly across his bloody lip.

And smiles.

Staring into my eyes.

Fucking smiling! Cassian doesn't smile. Ever.

Too far. I have pushed him too far and now the beast prowls free, he won't rein it back.

He's going to get us both killed.

24

LIVIA

Vitus doesn't falter from his orders. He works Cassian almost to the point of death.

Two whole days. No sleep. Minimal water. No food, save for the meagre amount of bread that I forced Alba to sneak to him.

Even the other gladiators wince when I approach. They fear me now. They fear me, because if I can sit back and let this happen to the gladiator I love, then I wouldn't hesitate to inflict far worse upon them.

Cassian is allowed one day of rest after his punishment, and then he's right back to rigorous training.

Marcus calls in briefly each day to check that everything is in order. He doesn't touch me again, but he does take delight in telling me that Felix will be staying away for longer on his trip, and that he will return in a few days for a more *thorough* inspection. My skin crawls.

I shake off the memory of those words, of the promise they hold, and summon Cassian to my room. The guard deposits him inside without so much as a glance at either of us.

I expect him to drop his head. To stare at my feet, or kneel before me, awaiting instruction. This is the way of things. The order.

But he does none of that. Instead, he marches straight for me and catches my throat in his hand. I don't even have time to let out a shriek. His grip tightens until I can barely breathe and shoves me back against the wall.

Piercing blue eyes shine vividly against the inky black of tattoos that creep up his neck, and consume his arms. Crystalline eyes, hiding a monster. He speaks against my mouth, "You fucking bitch. You want the beast? No problem. I will hate fuck that shit right out of you."

Kicking my feet apart, he hoists up my dress with his free hand. The other is still wrapped so firmly against my throat that I start seeing stars. Moving with predatory grace, he has his cock out in the next moment and it's pressing to my eager opening.

"You might be my Domina, you might control every person here," he says into my ear. "But right now, you are mine. I'm your master and you will worship at *my* feet. Do you understand?"

I try to nod. Or gargle. And he bites my ear. Claiming me. Marking me.

"Fail to satisfy me, whore, and I will break you, I will—" His words become lost to the roar of passion in my ears. He releases my throat and lifts me, wrapping my legs around his waist. Crushing my back into the wall again, he slams himself inside me.

I scream. And his hand comes back to clamp over my mouth.

"You will not scream unless I command it," he growls.

Whimpering, I buck against him, needing him deeper, needing more.

He pauses; another smile playing on his lips. So breathtaking. "Oh, you want more, do you?"

Nodding, I wriggle against him.

"Do you remember what happens when *I* want more? All the times you have denied me for your own selfish games?" He withdraws and stands back across the room, near the door. My chest tightens.

No, no, no. Don't leave me here, not like this.

I won't allow it. I'll command him... I will only play this game for so long...

Break him. Do not show weakness...

He stands before me, radiating carnal need. He isn't going anywhere, and that might scare me more. Breathing ragged. He stares me down with such ferocity that I'm both terrified and exhilarated.

Strong hands reach up to undo the buckle on his leather shoulder plate. He steps toward me, controlled, measured. One step. Two. All the while slowly pulling the strap away from the pauldron until he's left with a leather belt, which he draws through his fingers.

He wouldn't whip me. He can't... the marks it would leave...

Desire pools between my legs. So aching, so desperate. I'm pinned to the spot by the way he's looking at me. Dangerous. Sinful. Dirty.

Like I'm prey. Like he's going to devour me.

"Kneel," he orders, and my knees buckle.

I don't flinch when he puts the leather strap around my throat. Even though I'm immediately flooded by images of those dogs in the cage...

Break them. Tear them down.

Panic is rising. Panic that I'll never show.

He pauses. Waiting.

He won't hurt me. Not if I don't want it. I nod once, and slowly he eases the buckle tighter. The leather is cold and firm. Intimidating. "Good girl," he soothes, dragging a thumb down my cheek and into my mouth. "It's not so hard, is it?"

I shake my head, sucking his thumb and praying to the Gods that I'm not making a terrible mistake.

If you show weakness, they will destroy you.

Abruptly he yanks on the collar and manoeuvres me onto all fours.

I'm his bitch now. I moan my approval as his cock teases my wetness.

Then he slams home. Relentlessly. Hard and fast until I can't breathe.

He's a beast that can't be tamed. The very idea is absurd. He has been bred for this. He should never be tamed. It would be a tragedy to do so.

He's breathtaking. Savage. Beautiful. Just the way he should be.

I don't want him tamed. I want him just the way he is, in all his fucked-up glory.

25

CASSIAN

I want to hurt her. I *need* to...

I can't stop the hand that curls around her throat, and then her mouth, muffling her screams. I can't resist pulling on that collar, making her back arch, dragging her helpless body into mine. I want her to beg. To submit. I will give her the beast. Let's see how much she really likes it when she finds that the idea of an unhinged Thracian in her bed is much more thrilling than the reality.

Yet her delicious cunt is dripping with need. And her eyes are alive, for the first time in what feels forever. She's back. My Domina. Reckless and free, unbound.

I thrust into her like a starved creature, frantic for release. Harder. Faster.

Against the wall, then on the floor. Then I bend her over the bed once more and take her from behind, holding her hips and ploughing into that sweet core as if I may never see tomorrow.

In case I don't see tomorrow.

Any minute now the visions will come. They always do,

whenever I have sex. Except with her. When she makes love to me a silence sweeps through my veins. The fog lifts and the violence dies...

But now she has forced me into this. She has tortured and coaxed me, and now I'm fucking her like an animal, and the blood lust will surely come...

Thrusting, harder and deeper. I can't get deep enough. I throw her to her back on the floor and hoist a leg over my shoulder, angling to get deeper. Pulling her legs further apart.

Our love-making was my only sanity. But now she wants to take that only moment of peace from me, she wants to taint it by seeking the beast...

Palming her breasts, I squeeze and pull. I dig my nails into the thin scraping of flesh over her hips. I grab her everywhere, frantic and raw.

Sweat drips from my forehead. I didn't bathe before coming here straight from the training ground. Dusty and bloody. Her dirty, untamed animal.

She locks her eyes to mine and screams as her orgasm approaches.

"Come for me," I growl, withdrawing all the way out and slamming back in.

She cries out my name, over and over, as she tightens around my cock, pulsing and clenching. Bucking and arching, fingers clawing at me.

My hands go back to her throat, over the collar, and squeeze... tighter...

She flaps like a fish out of water, her body straining for breath. And I tumble into my own climax, spiralling down in a torrent of blissful release.

Dropping her leg, I collapse down beside her and stare at the ceiling.

The visions never came. The darkness never took hold. But I fucked her like a demon and loved every second.

26

LIVIA

I don't know how long we lay there, staring upwards. After a while, or an age, I turn and burrow into his chest. His arm wraps protectively around my body, tucking me in tighter.

Letting out a sigh, I open my mouth to speak.

"Please don't," he whispers. "Don't spoil it yet."

So I stroke his stomach lazily and wait... as long as I can bear before my head starts going crazy with the insistence that we can't lay there any longer.

"Aelia will tell Felix what really happened that night, in your cell," I say.

He huffs a noisy breath and removes himself from my clutches, grabbing his leathers.

"The threat is too great. We need her gone—"

"Gone?!" he shouts. "Dead?"

"We'll be the dead ones if we don't deal with her."

"You treat us with such contempt," he slams his fist into the table. "She's disposable to you, too? You can just have me fuck her and kill her, that simple?"

"There's no other way. Not now, with Marcus sniffing around, too. Everything is slipping..."

"Are you really *this* cold?" he shakes his head incredulously.

"Aren't you? You've killed a hundred people without remorse. What is the difference if I wish to kill one? You kill for survival, and perhaps, so shall I."

"You know nothing of my remorse. And you know nothing of killing."

"So teach me."

That did it. His fist coiled near my face as he considered striking.

"Am I really nothing more than a plaything to you? I understand that I'm your toy in the arena, I'm trained to perform for you there. But this? I don't understand this. Is it all a game?"

"You may devour my body, but you will not devour my heart," I say quietly.

"And yet, here I am, Domina, offering you mine on a silver platter."

"Is that what that was? Your heart?

He flinches as if I've struck him and I reach out to stroke his face, but he slaps my hand away.

"Every slave in this house knows what we do," his voice drops. "Your secret is never safe. Disposing of one girl does not fix that. Will you kill them all?"

My mouth opens and closes, but no words come out.

"You don't need to," he sighs, shaking his head. "The fact is, they will not betray you, because they will not betray *me*. I'm their family. We stick together. But if you wish to be certain of the secret remaining then it's a simple matter of treating them with respect. They live simple lives; all they ask for is a little kindness."

I try to speak again, but he cuts me off. “Call him. Now.”

I don’t know how the roles have reversed so dramatically, but I want to beg him to stay. Until I see the coldness in his eyes and find myself recoiling from it.

“Guard,” I croak.

The guard enters and Cassian drops his gaze, back to my feet. Submissive and broken. I watch a little piece of my heart escape as he is led from my room.

27

LIVIA

A few days have passed and I'm still wondering if I could really order an innocent slave girl killed? Cassian is still angry with me. I can see the way it thrums on him every time I'm near. So I leave him be. Once he's calmed down I'll call for him, but which gladiator will I receive? The submissive or the dominant? And which one do I want?

He's right, of course. Killing Aelia would cross a line, too far. Sending a gladiator to battle is one thing, but outright murder to try and protect myself is quite another. My head is a jumbled mess. I'm terrified. My feelings for Cassian are spiralling out of control and I don't know how to stop them.

I need him. He needs me.

But there's only one way this can end. We're living on borrowed time, waiting for our bubble to burst – our poisonous little bubble in which we just love to hurt each other. How long will it be before he snaps and kills me, as he would an opponent in the arena? He could do it so easily, and I know that sometimes he wants to.

He could have done it when he had that collar around my neck. I gave him all the power. I'm such a fool.

He's a slave. All he knows is hate and obedience towards his masters. Perhaps he only does what he does to humour me, to ensure he is of worth and that we keep him. Perhaps I am nothing but a spoiled rich bitch to him. He probably laughs with the other gladiators about me. The pathetic woman who can't keep her hands off the forbidden meat.

No.

No. I have seen the pain in his eyes, but I have also seen the love. I can't be the only one that feels this deep need—

"Livia!" Felix bellows through the villa.

Marcus never returned for his *thorough* inspection, because Felix arrived home this morning after all. I never thought there would come a day that I would be glad for his return, but this was that day. Even though I was now biting back fear and putting up every shield in readiness for what was to come.

I find him lying on the wooden couch, Aelia straddled over him, riding his cock with gusto. Titus stands, arms folded, watching the show with an expressionless face.

"Care to explain?" Felix asks, nodding to the fading bruises on her neck.

She darts a sideways glance at me and my heart freezes.

If she talks...

"You asked me to send a girl to your Champion, as his reward—"

"Do not take me for a fool, woman. You knew I did not mean *this* girl."

"Apologies," I mutter, beginning to remove my dress.

"Don't bother," he shakes his head in disgust. "Your jealousy of my Aelia is a massive turn-off. Take your bitter arse elsewhere, and be grateful that I do not have you flogged out there on the training ground."

I sag with relief and have to bite my tongue to keep from smiling.

The Gods have blessed me. I must find a way to repay them.

28

LIVIA

My mood is unusually light. I've cleared out the worry from my head. Felix didn't punish me for Aelia. Marcus never came back. And my gladiator recently owned me in a way that made my body sing and my mind turn to mush.

I flit around the villa and offer smiles to the slaves. They scurry away in confusion and I smile more. When I step outside even Cassian looks startled by my behaviour as he catches sight of me. He's dining at an outside table with the other men and quickly resumes eating but I pause, watching... waiting for the numerous glances in my direction. I pretend to be admiring the flowers that grow in our small garden below my balcony. Lingering. Pushing my luck.

One bit of good fortune and I'm courting danger again. Testing the boundaries further. Already dreaming up my next encounter with my gladiator. Perhaps he's right. Maybe if I give the slaves some kindness they'll continue to keep quiet and we won't have to end this... relationship.

Cassian finishes his meal and starts toward me, as if he's completely lost his mind, too. Vitus tugs his shoulder and redirects him to the cells. But not before he turns and flashes me a brooding glare over his shoulder. Still angry. It catches me so off guard that I shriek with surprise when Felix yells my name from within the villa.

He summons me to our balcony and we sit overlooking the courtyard. We come here to watch the gladiators training. My core thrums in approval at the thought of seeing Cassian out there today... rugged and swaggering, rigid with hateful passion for me. Oh yes, he will fight like a beast and I will swoon—

My heart stutters. It's not Cassian that appears on the ground below us, but Aelia. Bound and frightened.

Led by Titus, with death in his eyes.

"What is the meaning of this?" My voice trembles.

Felix glances at me with a ruthless smile. "This is about keeping the slaves in order."

Aelia is strapped to a large wooden cross in the centre of the grounds. I leave my seat and try to exit the balcony.

"Stay," Felix commands, pulling me back down.

This can't be happening. I spot Cassian stalking the courtyard perimeter. Up and down he prowls like a caged predator. Silent, stealthy... deadly. Just like the alpha dog used to...

He looks up to us in the balcony with a glare so defiant that I quickly take hold of Felix's hand to distract him. My palms grow clammy. "I don't understand, Aelia is your favoured girl—"

"She has been fucked by a gladiator. You've tainted her. She's of no worth to me now." He snatches back his hand and scans the yard. Mercifully Cassian is now locked in heated debate with Vitus.

My throat closes up. *You've tainted her.*

The first of her screams slaps me right in the face.

Quickly followed by another as Titus rips her clothing away and cracks a whip across her delicate back. The skin peels away as if it's nothing but silk.

"That wasn't her fault... she has committed no crime," I try to talk with conviction, but guilt swarms me, my voice falters.

It should be me, it should be me...

"You're right, it's not her fault, it's yours. Perhaps I should have you brandish the whip as your own punishment?"

I feel dizzy. I try to stand again.

"Sit down, woman!" he sighs. "Her punishment is deserved. She was stealing from me, every time we were together... a coin here, a coin there. It used to turn me on that she was so brazen, my brave little whore. Now she's just tainted. Let this be a lesson to the whole ludus that Felix Atticus will not tolerate their insolence."

She's screaming so loudly. Desperate and agonised. The sound of each strike echoes through my skull.

29

LIVIA

Felix is long gone. As are Cassian and Vitus.

Titus was the last to leave. He ran his hands over her limp body, mocking her, celebrating her death. Wickedness laced his every movement. Honestly, I think if he hadn't noticed me still watching from the balcony then he might have spent the whole day playing with his dead toy.

I sit here, staring at her, and emptiness threatens to swallow me. I can't stop replaying it over and over in my mind. The whip, the sound, the look on her face... the overzealous beating from Titus that ripped the light from her eyes.

It's been hours, but I can't move. I can't tear my attention away.

Not even when the crows come to peck at her glazed eyes. Going for the softest, juiciest parts first; so Felix informed me once.

I will keep this image with me forever. My own punishment. Every day I will see her dead face and remember that *I did this.* How could I ever have suggested that we kill her? Was I truly no better than my husband?

I held their lives in my palm and watched so many fade from existence before me. How many gladiators had I sent into the arena? How many men had I seen die? And how many times had I enjoyed it?

All the time.

But not this time. This time, something broke inside me.

30

LIVIA

It's only when night has fallen and I can no longer see her that I venture through the villa in search of Alba. I don't know how I will look at her, without feeling every ounce of her blame and hatred, but I must try. I must say something to her. They were friends...

As I pass his private room I hear Felix talking with Marcus from within. I pause, just around the door, and hold my breath.

"He's a liability," Marcus speaks. "He has too much confidence and position within this ludus. It's only a matter of time before he rebels and brings you strife."

"He's my best fighter," Felix mumbles.

"His performance at the last games was terrible. If he has another fight like that then his value will drop beyond repair. There are plenty more out there. Sell him and choose another."

"It's not that simple—"

"Know that if he disrespects me again, I will have him killed. I don't care that he's your champion. Then you'll be left with no money out of him at all. Get rid of him, now."

There's a pause, and my heart stops in case they've realised I'm here, but then Marcus speaks again. "Have you seen the way he looks at your wife?"

"What?" Felix shouts.

No!

No, no, no.

Panic claws up my spine.

"You've seen it," Marcus replies. "Will you seriously continue to ignore it?"

"He's a dirty animal with no intelligence. He poses no threat to me."

Marcus laughs. "He poses *every* threat to you, brother. Do not dismiss his capabilities just because you think you have him shackled. Is Aelia not warning enough? The minds of these savages can only be contained for so long—"

"I've had an offer," Felix interrupts. "Erucias has offered me a large sum of coin if I have Cassian throw a fight. He's looking to improve the ranking of his own gladiator and happy to pay to ensure his victory."

"It better be a lot of coin to make that worthwhile. Having your gladiator surrender will render him worthless from there on. You'd have to throw him away to pit fighting after a defeat like that. Then you'd never sell him, you'll still be stuck with him here—"

"I'm not talking about having him surrender. He'll be instructed to endure a total defeat. Erucias will have his man kill Cassian."

"Well," Marcus muses. "That would certainly be a fitting punishment."

The room darkens at the edges.

My legs wobble, and my head hits the stone floor with a crack.

There's nothing but black.

31

LIVIA

I come round in my bed with Alba mopping my brow.

Of course Felix wasn't there, hovering in worry to check on his wife like a normal husband. No. He was elsewhere, and when Alba called him to say that I'd awoken, it still took him an age to arrive, adjusting his manhood back into place beneath his tunic. Did he fuck all day long?

Trying to sit up, a blinding wave of pain shoots through my head. I touch my fingers to the dried blood in my hair.

"It's only a minor wound, Domina," Alba pats my leg.

"What's the matter with you?" Felix demands.

"I don't know... I was just walking to the kitchen and I felt dizzy..."

"You're not with child are you?"

"No." *No!* Gratitude to the Gods, the secret tonic I took each day seemed to be preventing that.

"Are you sick?" No concern in his voice, only annoyance.

"No," I sigh.

"Very well, then. Try eating more food, you're a bag of old bones these days."

"Yes, I will." Alba's hand tightens on my knee. A gesture

that seemed like one of support. Why would she offer me any sort of comfort?! Maybe she was grateful for the time I let her have with Vitus. Though she was a fool if she couldn't see that I only did it for my own benefit.

For time spent with Cassian—

Erucias will have his man kill Cassian...

I can't breathe.

I reach up to my throat, feeling the colour drain from my face.

I'm going to be sick.

I lean over the side of the bed and vomit all over the floor.

Felix backs out of the room. "For fuck's sake. I'm going away to the other villa, I don't want to catch whatever sickness you harbour. Send word to me once you have recovered."

Alba nods and he pauses in the doorway. "Oh, and Albina—"

"Alba," I correct.

He glares at us. "*Alba*, I know that you've been going against house rules and having sexual relations with Vitus. And furthermore, that it has been going on for many months. I don't care who my lanista fucks to release his tensions, but I will not have him falling in love. You will be flogged and sent to live with my brother. Marcus has shown great interest in putting you to work in the privacy of his own villa." He sneers and my stomach recoils, threatening to empty again.

"Husband, I implore you. Alba is my best maid—"

"Find another."

"But... but only last week she confided in me that Vitus has lost interest in her," I lie, calling after him. "Their relationship is no threat to his work."

"It is done. Marcus will collect her once she's finished nursing you back to health."

And then he's gone.

Alba's wild eyes flit from me to the floor. Her hand has gone bone white as it grips my leg.

"I'm sorry. I'll try again. I'll do whatever I can to change his mind."

"I'm sorry, too," she whispers, and I curl into myself on the bed.

32

LIVIA

I sleep. And sleep.

Days pass and I don't move from my room.

I can't face him. How can I? How could I look upon those beautiful blue eyes, upon that body that seemed built only for me, and not break apart into a thousand pieces?

He wouldn't be able to refuse the order from his Dominus. If he did, he would only be executed anyway, but with extra shame and dishonour. Felix would find a way to strip him of everything he held dear, his pride, his honour... he would make him suffer.

To surrender in battle is shameful. Weak.

To die at the hands of a better opponent, going down fighting – that is the glory they all hope to achieve when their time is up.

But to die because you have been told to fail. To deliberately fall and allow a weaker man to kill you. This would be the worst end imaginable to a warrior like Cassian.

In fact, I realise that he would rather take whatever else Felix would throw at him. He'd square his shoulders and endure it. Anything but that hideous, weak death.

Death.

I heave, but nothing comes up because I've not eaten for days.

I can't lose him.

I can't.

I won't let him go.

33

CASSIAN

She stumbles across the courtyard. An apparition. Her flaming hair burning brightly in the sunlight against her ashen skin. Her face is gaunt. Sunken.

Tears stream down her cheeks.

She knows.

Her legs begin to buckle and she looks like she'll collapse.

I run to her, ignoring the shouts from Vitus, and scoop her into my arms.

Let them all see. I'm beyond caring. If I am to die anyway, then what does it matter?

It matters for her sake, you fool! You don't have to sentence her to death along with yourself.

But I can't stop myself. I can't hold back the kiss that I plant on her cheek, tasting the salt from her tears.

Vitus is yelling at me like a deranged imbecile. They all are. They all yell and swear and gesture for me to put her down.

But I don't. I kiss her lips this time and she whimpers.

Then I carry her into my cell and hold her tight.
Fuck this.
Fuck them all.

34

CASSIAN

"You've lost your mind," she giggles. Delirious. When did she last eat?

I brush a strand of hair from her sticky cheek. "I lost it a long time ago, Domina."

She laughs loud and free. Then a sob breaks through and she cries into my shoulder. I hold her until she has no more tears left.

"This is all my fault." Her voice is barely more than a whisper.

"Yes."

"Why didn't Aelia tell Felix what I did that night in your cell?"

"There would have been no honour in that. She stood nothing to gain from betraying you. He'd have killed her regardless."

"She wasn't a gladiator, what did she know of dying with honour?"

A wisp of anger curls through my fists. "Honour is not something only reserved for us! If a supposed savage can die with that grace, then should everyone else not be able to manage the same?"

Her head bows. I could teach her so much, if only she would open the doors wide enough to let me in.

But she did this. I want her to suffer. Then a heartbeat later, I want to take every bit of suffering she has ever endured and erase it. I will take her pain for her. I am her gladiator. I will die for her. Willingly.

"When is the fight?" she asks, as if reading my mind, and a piece of my soul breaks away.

"Tomorrow."

Her answering wail has me clamping her into my chest to reduce the noise. I don't wait for her to finish this time. Instead, I place a finger under her chin and lift her face to mine. Then I run my tongue along her bottom lip, and kiss her through the tears.

There are no more words to say. There are none that can make a difference now. We both knew this couldn't last forever.

And so we don't speak. But we kiss, and we kiss, and when our lips are too swollen for any more, I remove her tunic and worship her body. I don't miss a single bit of her. Every exquisite part of her soft skin receives kisses and licks, until she rolls us over and offers me the same.

Hours pass in this way before I finally give in and slide myself inside her. The explosion of relief shatters us both. She cries again and I stare deep into her eyes, rocking slowly back and forth.

We make love right through the night and into the dawn.

35

LIVIA

Vitus can't look at me, even when I command him to. None of them can.

They all know the fate that awaits Cassian today, and they all bear the shame and grief with him. Their sad eyes track the Champion as he chooses his armour and readies himself. I can't bear the tension any longer. I will suffocate. I can barely even stand...

Marcus arrives through the gates and marches onto the courtyard with a bounce in his step, looping an arm through mine.

"Livia!" he delights. "Felix has asked me to escort you to the games. I trust you're not sick any longer?" He casts a backward glance at Cassian and for a moment I wish that the gladiator would just do it. Let him strike Marcus down right now.

But he doesn't. And my balance falters again. I can't go. I can't go and watch this...

"Actually, I'm still not well," I mutter.

Cassian coughs loudly from behind and I stop to look

back. He has already fixed his gaze back on the weapons, but I know what he meant. He wants me to go. He needs me there.

I swallow the bile in my throat and smile weakly at Marcus. “But, I’m sure I’ll be fine. Let’s go.”

36

LIVIA

I couldn't say what happened in the hours since leaving the ludus. I don't remember any of it. It's just people, faces, noise... none of it makes it through the barrier that I've erected.

Do not show weakness.

I will endure this the only way I know how – by shutting it out. By locking myself down and embracing the numbness.

Cassian's fight has begun. They've shared blows back and forth, whipping up the crowd.

It's too obvious that Cassian is a far better fighter. When he stumbles and allows the blow... when he allows that sword to swipe over his arm, drawing a wound... my heart stops and I wonder how on earth the crowd can't see that it's fake, that he's backing down.

His opponent, a Thraex fighter, swaggers to the other side of the arena, pumping his sword in the air like he's already won. From one little nick to the arm. I can see the way Cassian's jaw clenches, the way he wants to cut that smile from his enemy's face.

I can't do this. I can't watch...

Panic surges through me.

I would rather die than watch this happen. The barrier is slipping...

The Thraex lunges and Cassian forces himself to dodge too slowly, the sword nicking at his side this time.

The fight has been going on too long. The crowd grow weary of the minor injuries, of the to and fro. As does Felix, nervous on the edge of his seat. The booing begins and Cassian's shoulders seem to cave. He could have finished this battle long ago. One attack and the opponent would be dead.

Just one feint and swipe. *Please, Cassian...*

But the jeering from the crowd is deafening, and the next time the Thraex makes his weak attack, Cassian crumbles and falls. His opponent stands over him, a foot planted on his chest.

The crowd cheer.

Felix readies himself to pretend that he is shocked and angered.

A sword is lifted high, ready to swing down onto my gladiator.

My love.

Cassian was not made to walk amongst men, much less to serve them. He belongs with the Gods. Mighty, brave, fierce, loyal.

The Thraex takes a deep breath, lifting higher. He looks to his official for approval, which they grant him with a nod.

And I scream.

It erupts from my mouth in a torrent that I can't call back. Cassian's head whips round to find me. The world stills. Time has stopped.

His eyes catch mine and I know... he's everything. He always was.

Felix clamps a hand over my mouth and Cassian snarls. The blade begins its downward arc, but he rolls out of the way. It strikes the sand and Cassian leaps to his feet. With one furious swipe he cuts the Thraex's head clean from his shoulders.

Blood erupts like rain, drenching him. The crowd go wild. And Felix goes still. The promise of death seeping from his pores.

37

LIVIA

Marcus puts a hand under Felix's arm and pulls him to his feet.

"For fuck's sake, Felix, smile. Your gladiator just won. Clap your hands and cheer. Do you want the whole amphitheatre to suspect any wrong-doing?" Marcus speaks through gritted teeth.

I catch sight of the Thraex owner – fuming. He has paid my husband to fix this fight and now he'll want compensation.

Felix whispers in my ear, "Whatever is going on, there will be punishments the likes of which you couldn't even conjure in your nightmares." Then he applauds and smiles for the crowds.

My heart swells with relief. Cassian is alive!

Then it dies.

He has sealed our fates. And they will be filled with horror.

38

LIVIA

The after-game reception banquet is to go ahead as scheduled.

But the plan had always been that we would return to the villa in defeat. That our prized gladiator would be dead, and we would be mourning our loss and looking to buy another.

Felix wanted to cancel the event. He wanted to get back here alone and have everyone beaten to a bloody pulp. Me, Cassian, Vitus... all of us. Then he would work out how he planned to kill us.

Marcus, though, had reminded him that eyes were on us right now. Our Champion had endured and if Felix did not act in the appropriate way then he risked raising suspicion. Punishments would have to wait until the party had finished and the dust had settled.

So the villa fills with nobles from all over Rome. And our gladiators stand in a line; there to be studied and enjoyed, sneered at and marvelled. They stand for hours – hands clasped, heads bowed, allowing the ladies to come and touch them, to giggle as they grip their firm muscles and swoon.

I've spent my life training for this existence. Having it ground into me how a lady behaves, what her wifely duties involve, and how to position myself in society amongst the rich and powerful. How to indulge in the same games. I know my place here. I understand the rank and reasoning.

Just as surely as the slaves have trained for their futures. Taught to bow and scrape, and never look up. Never to hold their heads high and look upon the world with confidence.

And yet, I find myself wondering if I'm really so different, after all? If my freedom really means anything, when I'm so tied and controlled. An empty life and an empty heart.

Perhaps the slaves are richer than me. They still have hope, and love?

Break them. Then build them up...

I no longer feel like I belong with these people. I don't understand them.

But I try. I mingle, and I smile, and I bury every aching part of my heart into a place where I can't feel it.

I should be happy that Cassian didn't die. That I can perhaps have another day or two. But his punishment now will surely be far worse, and I think it will kill me, too.

As the evening draws on Felix orders a fight in the courtyard. Everyone chants and laughs as some of our men carry out a choreographed battle.

Cassian is not permitted to move from his stage. The star of the show. Cleaned of his opponent's blood, but still looking like he'd survived a war. The deep wound on his arm has been dressed. The one on his side is left raw, to add further spice and excitement when viewing him.

He doesn't dare look at me, not once. How it burns to

have his eyes on the floor tonight, knowing how it feels to have them greedily feasting upon me. Knowing what terror lay ahead for us all and wanting so desperately for his gaze to reassure me, to let me know it would be alright.

But it couldn't be, and we all knew it. Vitus and Alba had begun to take on the presence of sacrificial offerings; sad sunken eyes, rapid breathing, awaiting the slaughter. Defeated. The tension in the air was suffocating.

And he knew it. Felix knew exactly how we tip-toed through the evening, watching him, waiting for the explosion. He drank his wine and lapped it up.

39

LIVIA

My friend, Camilla, is at the party. I had almost forgotten I even have friends. Too consumed, too lost in my own little world to even think of them.

"You seem preoccupied these days, my love. I've barely seen you for months. Is everything well?" Camilla leans forward to inspect my face. As if she will find anything there. I'm too good at hiding behind this bland expression.

Felix spares me from having to answer when he stumbles over in a drunken state. "Look at the way the women paw over our Champion, Livia," he grins, and I turn as casually as I can to see one of the said women cupping Cassian's balls beneath the flimsy leather flap. His face is set, dead calm, indifferent – not a flicker of emotion. But my indifference almost falters. I dig a nail into my palm.

"You know," Felix continues, "I'm thinking I might make an announcement. Let's offer up the sexual services of our Cassian for the night. The highest bidders get to bed the wild beast in the safety of our villa. Perhaps they can use our bed?" He cuts me with an icy glare. I swallow and force my face into neutrality.

"Yes, a fine idea," he slurs to himself. "After all, I need all the extra coin I can get with a wife like you. You're like a leech. Sucking onto my cock for dear life to keep a fine roof over your head. Coin grabbing whore..." He lurches away with those words, over to Cassian... over to the women...

I watch as he talks and they gasp and clutch at their breasts in shock. Then, shyly, they reach to their bags for their money.

"I bet even the married ones will bed him tonight," Marcus comments as he passes by. "What a thrill for a husband to watch his wife fucked into submission by such a brute."

I cough and try desperately to stop my hands from shaking. Marcus melts back into the party.

"Why do you tolerate your husband being such a cunt?" Camilla asks, perusing Cassian with interest.

"I have little choice," I say between gritted teeth. "I'm grateful to have him. Lucky—"

"You keep telling yourself that and you might start believing it soon."

"What would you suggest? That I stand up to him and have to face his punishments, having gained nothing? If I walk out that door then it's with shame upon my shoulders and no money. What man worth anything would take me in?"

"True. That's why you must find a new man before leaving that shrivelled old goat. Men always covet what they can't have. If something is deemed precious to one man, then others want it for themselves. So go out there with a sparkle in your eye, show them you're happy, offer the shy smiles and winks... they'll soon be tripping over themselves for an affair with you. Then it's just a matter of time and manipulation before you can run off into the sunset with them."

"Time is something I'm running out of," I groan. My nails dig deeper into my palms and I watch the horror on Cassian's face as he's led away with an excited woman in tow.

"Or, how about this for an idea... maybe you don't need a man?" Camilla gasps playfully.

I force out a laugh. And so does she. But she soon stops when she notices the way I can't breathe.

"So here's one more idea, and it's my favourite," she whispers, taking my hand in hers. "Kill him."

I spit my drink into my lap.

"You'll get his money and he'll be gone—"

"I think you've had enough wine for today," I mumble and hurry away.

40

LIVIA

I look in every room trying to find Cassian, but he's nowhere. And nor is that woman.

This is bad. So very bad. It will push him over the edge. If he's forced into sex with these women then his visions will come... who knows what he might do to them.

I don't find Cassian, but I do find an orgy in just about every room. Wine has flowed and inhibitions have faded. I drift from one scene to another, dodging the invitations to join in. The night feels like it will never end. But then, I don't want it to. As long as this night continues, Cassian still lives... I hope.

Rounding a corner, I bump into Marcus. He has Alba pinned against the wall, a hand between her legs. Tears in her eyes.

"Alba," I croak. "Your services are required in the banquet hall—"

"Her services are no longer anything to do with you. Alba belongs to me and will be moving into my villa tonight." Marcus gives her a vile grin.

Her eyes widen. Lips tremble.

"Well, if you'll be having your fill of her from now on then why do you need her now? I'm sure we could find our own entertainment for tonight..." I trail a hand along his chest.

"Livia, Livia," he smirks. "You're jealous?"

I smile meekly and he turns to slobber into my neck. "I knew you craved my attention," his voice is a rancid breath on my ear. Every part of me wants to shrivel away from his touch, but I lean in closer and glare over his shoulder at Alba.

Go!

She hesitates, and then darts away.

After sticking his tongue down my throat for what seems an eternity, Marcus yanks me through to the main room to say goodbye to our guests. Many of them have already drifted away. A few are left, bingeing themselves on the last dregs of wine and food. He clears his throat and makes a few comments about people overstaying their welcome.

I still can't see Cassian anywhere. The urge to run from room to room in a hunt for him is so overpowering that I have to grip a table to root myself in place.

Felix suddenly swaggers into the fray, a giggling girl on each arm. "I'm going to spend the rest of the night at my other villa," he announces, to anyone listening.

As he leaves, Marcus rushes over and presses a bag of coins into Felix's hand, talking animatedly in his ear. Felix nods, and drags his prey out the door.

Marcus turns to smile at me.

I already know what the money was for. I needn't have offered myself to Marcus to protect Alba, because my husband just sold me to him like a common whore.

41

LIVIA

The guests have all gone. Cassian is nowhere to be found. Vitus and Alba have disappeared. All of the gladiators are back in their barracks.

It's just me, and Marcus.

He sniggers as he drags me to my room. Then he turns abruptly and clenches my chin between his fingers, squeezing until I cry out in pain. "Do you think your husband knows you fuck his gladiators?"

"Gladiator. Single. And does your wife know that you fuck your brother's bride? Or that the new maid you've acquired will be there to open up for your pathetic cock—" He slaps me around the face and my head whips over my shoulder.

A rumbling growl, barely even sounding human, comes from the adjoining bathing room. Alarm causes me to gasp, visions of wild dogs... but Marcus merely smiles.

Cassian appears in the doorway. Fresh lashings from a whip adorn his chest. One strike has even split open his cheek, narrowly missing his eye.

Marcus saunters over and pats him on the shoulder like

a pet dog. "Ahh, Cassian," he grins, and then turns to me. "We've come to an agreement, your *Champion*, and me."

Breathing becomes hard again.

"Felix is very intent upon a plan of torture and death for this barbarian, but I might have found a willing buyer and convinced him that the coin from such a sale far outweighs the satisfaction of revenge."

"Why?" I take a step back, needing to feel the wall behind me to stop from falling.

"Why?" Marcus breezes. "Because Cassian here would rather be sold to another than die. He's no fool. In return for this favour that I bestow upon him, he will perform for me tonight. He will indulge in my every sexual whim between the three of us."

Cassian's eyes flash with rage.

"Horse-shit," I spit. "He's a Thracian warrior. He would rather die than sell those services to you."

Marcus bites his lower lip. "Very astute. I might also have sweetened the deal by ensuring the death of his Domina unless he plays along. Considering you are mine now—"

Cassian's swearing causes Marcus to duck away like a frightened child. Then he laughs nervously. "I can see your attraction, Livia. Thrilling, isn't it? Having such a savage under your control."

Cassian takes a step forward but I shake my head at him. The pleading in his eyes near breaks me. *No*. I shake my head again.

Marcus claps his hands. "Then let's begin."

42

LIVIA

"Remove her robes," Marcus sits on the bed and issues his first command.

Cassian walks to me with sorrow on his face, but I offer him a smile. This will be alright. Because he will live. Yes, he will be sold and I will lose him, but he will *live!* There can be no better offer.

I trace my finger along his jaw and plant a kiss to his lips.

"I didn't say to fucking kiss like lovers!" Marcus snorts. "You are a savage, you will brutalise this woman."

I step out of the kiss and allow Cassian to pull my dress away. Every moment his jaw clenches tighter. He can't do this. He won't...

You must do this! I silently plead.

When I'm naked, Marcus barks his next demand. "Bend her over this bed and spank her ass."

I walk to the bed and position myself. "Not there," he shouts. "Here." He grabs my hair and pulls me so that I'm bent over with my head at his groin. He adjusts his clothing and his cock springs into my face. I don't even get the chance to think about what Cassian will do, before Marcus has pressed his erection to my mouth.

I think that Cassian will erupt. But instead I feel the sharp whip of his hand landing on my backside.

Thank the Gods! You can do this Cassian. You must...

A second thwack, and I start sucking on Marcus. He groans in absolute delight and I sag with relief. This will work. Cassian will live and I will endure.

43

LIVIA

It's all a blur, as these things often are. Every vile word to spew from Marcus's lips, every time he makes me lick him, every time his cock thrusts into me. I keep my attention firmly on Cassian as often as I can, but I can see how much more it breaks his heart when I'm looking at him. But it's my only solace through the pain. His rugged, determined face is my safe place.

Just keep looking at him and reminding myself that this will all be worth it.

But Marcus is pushing too far. Demanding too much. Cassian brims with so much rage that for a moment I have to admire the bravery in Marcus. Of course though, it's not bravery. It's sheer arrogance. He thinks himself a better man, more worthy. Accustomed to getting what he wants in every step of life. He's untouchable and relishing in his power.

They all are. All these noble men and women across Rome. And I'm one of them. I'm no better. Just a high-ranking pig, controlling the lives of others as if I'm a Goddess.

But I am not. Right here, right now, I'm nothing. I've always just been nothing.

Cassian is far more worthy than any of us. He has honour and pride, and compassion. How much more of this will he tolerate?

As if reading my mind, Marcus suddenly exits the room and returns barely a moment later brandishing shackles. How long had he planned this?

He instructs Cassian and keeps a wary eye on him while he binds his hands and feet. Cassian then slumps to the floor and braces himself for the show.

Marcus is just getting going, ploughing into me like a squealing hog, when a commotion from the courtyard catches our attention.

"What's going on?" I ask. Cassian stiffens.

"Probably my guard come to collect Alba from the desperate clutches of your lanista," Marcus waves a hand in dismissal. "And to collect Cassian. I did tell you that the buyer for your gladiator is myself, right?"

Silence engulfs my mind, swallowing all the noise, even that of my thrashing heart. Pure, hateful silence. This couldn't be. Marcus would subject us both to a lifetime of this agony...

He laughs, wild and free and crazed. "I rather like the idea of owning a gladiator in the bedroom as well as the arena. You know what?" He abruptly withdraws from me. "I think I'd like to experiment. Stand up, Cassian."

Cassian does as instructed, slowly, warily.

"Now bend over and spread your cheeks. Look at your worthless Domina while I fuck you in the ass like the mongrel you are."

No!

No no no no...

44

LIVIA

Too much.

This is too much.

Cassian tugs on his restraints. Marcus laughs and moves behind him. As he turns I grab a heavy vase from the table and whack it into his skull. He lands on the floor with a dull thud.

Cassian and I just stare at each other in horror.

I dig my toe into Marcus's ribs and he twitches. I can still hear the commotion outside. Raised voices, scuffling. His guard could arrive here any second. Cassian is tugging against his shackles again and I launch into action.

Marcus groans.

I fumble with Cassian's bindings, my hands shaking.

"Breathe," he soothes.

"I can't!" I scream, yanking at the strap that won't loosen.

Marcus stirs again, his hands twitching to life at his sides. Blood pools beneath his head, but he's definitely not dead.

He's not dead. I should feel relief.

"Will you kill for me? For us?" I blurt out, as the final restraint falls away.

"Is that not what I do every time I step in the arena?"

"Now. Here—"

"I'm yours to command, Domina, no matter when or where." Cassian reaches out to embrace me and I fall into his safe arms. I'm secure against his warmth, and yet his touch will be the bringer of death upon us all.

I look to the corner. Look to the floor... under the bed.

Marcus tries to sit up and Cassian doesn't waste another second.

He lurches for the bed and grabs the knife hidden underneath.

45

CASSIAN

Rage.

Unlike anything I've ever encountered.

There's nothing – no voices in my head, no sound from Livia's lips, no world beyond the doors. There is only me, and him, and my wrath. Blinding and hot.

I grab Marcus's hair and press the knife to his throat.

Fear sparks behind his eyes as he wakes fully and comprehends his fate. This man spends his time thinking he's an emperor, prowling his domain, abusing women against their wishes and pushing slaves around. Revelling in the destruction caused by his gladiators. It's just games.

But he is not a strong man. He's weak. Hiding behind his wealth. He has no idea how to take a life himself. And now he's here... facing the unshackled monster. No guards to protect him. And he's just pissed himself. Literally.

If he hadn't pushed so far he might have got away with it. Might have lived another day.

I side-step away from the puddle on the floor, maintaining my hold on him. I should take it slow. I should cut him up piece by piece, one body part at a time. I would enjoy that.

But I look to my owner, as I would in the arena, and await her command.

She nods her head, and I slit his throat.

46

LIVIA

It's gone quiet outside.

It's gone quiet again in my head.

Marcus's blood spurted out like a fountain, drenching Cassian's chest. He stands there, shoulders heaving, the knife hanging limply in his hand. I'm drawn to his tattoos, the way they circle and creep around his arms. The way they look so black and solid against the silky red splatters that coat his skin.

My whole body surges with adrenalin. Alive. Alive...

"We need to clean this up. Somehow. I don't know—" Cassian starts moving around the room, pacing.

I get myself in front of him and he stops.

We won't be alive much longer.

I dab a finger to the blood, marvelling at the hot stickiness of it. Then I swipe it over the whorl of a tattoo, dragging across his solid muscles. He takes a deep breath. "Domina, —"

"Ssshhh," I soothe, leaning in to lick the smear of blood. His whole body tightens as a whoosh of air escapes his lungs. "Let us unleash the sickness. Let us be free."

He goes to reply, but I'm already palming his crotch and biting his neck. On a starved growl he throws me to the ground and plunges into my heat. My back slides against the pool of crimson death around us. I let it cover my hands before reaching up to stroke him, to rub it all over.

We are broken. Sick and depraved. Starved of love. And so we fuck like animals beside Marcus's dead body.

47

LIVIA

This time, it's definitely too quiet outside. Marcus's guard should have come looking for him by now.

I extract myself from Cassian's slumbering grip and shake myself into motion. We might have accepted our fates, but we could still try... do something...

Pulling Cassian along, we tumble through the house and out to the courtyard. We don't have many guards, but there's one stationed by the barracks. He takes in the state of us, naked and covered in blood, and reaches for his weapon.

"I wouldn't," Cassian warns.

The guard backs down with a huff. "This night has already gone to total shit," he mumbles. "You realise that you and your lanista have condemned us all, this whole ludus? No one will escape punishment." He gestures us through and we find Vitus cradling a sobbing Alba.

In the corner, a man lays dead. Marcus's guard.

Vitus has lost all the light in his eyes. "He tried to take her... I couldn't..."

"It's alright," I breathe.

But it wasn't alright. None of this was alright.

"We need to flee," Cassian states. Vitus nods in agreement. The other gladiators have gathered around us. A united front.

"To where?" I counter. "The city cohorts will be after us in a heartbeat."

"We're more than capable of taking on a few guards," Cassian scoffs, and the other men grunt approval.

I take a calming breath. "You would have me live in poverty? Always running, afraid, hungry?"

He looks at me incredulously. "What of the alternative?! You would rather die?"

Yes. I would rather die than live in poverty like a slave...

No.

That was the old Livia. The Domina.

This is a new me. One who is not afraid to take hold of what I want. With death loitering right over my head, the usual numbness has faltered. A fierce passion to live has broken through.

"I will protect you, to the ends of the earth," Cassian's face softens.

"Maybe I shall protect you, gladiator," I smile, and the ludus gates creak open.

48

LIVIA

Birdsong flits over the grounds as little wings take flight against the disturbance from the gates. Morning had broken at some point. Why were we still sitting here? If we were going to flee, it should have been under the cover of nightfall.

And I realise then – they would have fled. Cassian would have gone hours ago. But he would not leave without me. And he would not drag me like a prisoner. The longer I had lingered over my own foolish fears, the closer I had brought our doom.

"Go," I urged. "I'll keep him distracted while you gather enough supplies, then meet me by the ludus gates."

Cassian shakes his head.

"You must, I'll be fine, I promise." I throw a bowl of water over myself and scrub frantically at the dried blood that's glued to my skin.

The footfall of a horse and cart approaches the villa. Alba tears off her tunic and throws it to me. I hastily dry myself with a rag from the cell and pull on the dress.

Cassian catches my arm. The horse draws ever closer. "Please, Cassian, it's our only chance."

His hand is locked on me. Anguish. Fear.

"She's right," Vitus says, urging Cassian away.

"He will have been drunk and fucking all night long," I force a smile. "It won't take long before he'll collapse and fall asleep. I'll meet you then."

I don't wait for Cassian to grab me again. I sprint for the house and throw myself onto the wooden couch, just a moment before Felix walks in.

49

LIVIA

My breath is too rapid. My appearance too flustered. Flecks of blood still speckle my arms if you look closely enough.

Count, up and down. Deep breaths. Do not show weakness.

Felix trips over a discarded sandal and attempts to kick it away, only stumbling further and muttering obscenities. Still drunk.

Titus looms in the doorway. Fear engulfs me—

But Vitus appears, calm and collected, and asks Titus to join him for a word. Felix waves them away without a second thought.

Catching sight of the left over feast on the table, he strolls over and begins picking at the food. He scoffs down a platter of meat and half a cup of wine before turning and catching sight of me for the first time since entering.

"Marcus finished with you, has he?" he sneers. "You look terrible. I trust it was an experience."

"You sold me to him." I don't know why it hurts.

"Only for one night, don't start bleating about it, my head hurts enough already." He gulps back the rest of the wine. "Where is he, anyway? Has he returned home with Alba already? Not that I could blame him, she's far perkier than you—"

"Yes, he left. Right after he laughed about what an incompetent fool his brother is." His lip twitches, so I continue. "About how easy you are to manipulate. How he'll always be the one in charge. I mean, fucking his brother's wife?! Does he let you fuck his own bride? Does he let you make any of his business decisions? No..."

I stand to get myself some wine and steady my nerves, and his foot swipes at my ankle, sending me flying down. My temple cracks against the fireplace as I fall. Then sweaty hands are grabbing at my face and hair. He yanks my head up and smashes it back down into the mosaic floor. Light bursts behind my eyelids and I struggle to keep from drifting out of consciousness.

Fingers tighten, pulling hair from the roots. "What did you say, you miserable whore?" He prepares to crack my skull again. I frantically scramble around until my fingers find the iron poker for the fire.

My head is lifted high up from the ground. I find his eyes, hateful and cold, and brace for the impact. But the poker is in my grip and I stab the sharp point into his side. His shocked face is so empowering, I wish I could freeze it and admire it for hours. But it soon crumples into pain and fear. He falls back on his ass, clutching at the bleeding wound.

"That's for Aelia," I mutter.

I crawl to him, my head spinning, and before he can realise what I mean to do I stab again into the top of his chest. He falls flat onto his back, gasping. "And that one's for Cassian."

Horror in his expression now. It's beautiful. My heart

soars. I stand over him and slowly wipe the bloodied poker across my tunic. My insides are churning, but my hands are steady.

I will never show weakness.

The lesser men must know their place. I had it all wrong for so long. Cassian is the real man, the one who deserves respect. This man... he is not even worthy of the title of man.

Blood bubbles from his lips. He's trying to say something, but I can't make it out.

"And this one? This one is for me." I bring the pole down, right into his throat.

I am free.

50

LIVIA

I will never be free. I will most likely be imprisoned or dead before this day ends.

And if not, then I'll be bound by the restrictions of a life in poverty, a life in hiding...

And I don't care.

I charge toward the gates, passing the wooden cross in the centre of the grounds. It's no longer Aelia's body that hangs there – it's Titus. Nailed to the wood. Crucified and twitching. He lifts his bloody face to stare at me, but I fix my focus on Cassian – standing by the gates.

As soon as his eyes meet mine I know; I will never need anything else. What a terrible crime it is that I made him look at my feet for so long. His steel gaze upon me takes my breath away.

I have hastily washed again and pulled on fresh clothing. One of the bags I carry contains everything I could cram in, in terms of clothing and anything of value. The other bag is bulging with all the money that Felix kept locked away in his private room. Unfortunately, he keeps most of his wealth guarded by a bank, but Vitus's eyes still widen when he takes the bag from me and realises what's inside. It seems like a lot to them, but it's not enough...

Vitus lets out a sigh, dumping the bags into a cart. The horse fidgets impatiently against the harness. "Thank the Gods you're here, I couldn't hold Cassian back any longer from coming to find you."

"He's sleeping?" Cassian asks.

"Yes. Deeply asleep," I smile.

"Good. Then let's hope he burns slowly." Cassian turns to face the villa with a nod, and two gladiators hurry back to it.

"A fire might cover up the murders and allow us more time to flee," Vitus adds.

We watch in silence. Waiting. Before long a wisp of smoke drifts from my balcony.

51

LIVIA

I plead with Vitus and Alba to come with us, even some of the other gladiators, surely there's more safety in numbers? But they all have the same response.

"No, it will be more dangerous together." A group looking like ours will draw too much attention. We are to disperse. Disappear.

We will sneak through towns and run. We won't look back. We won't falter.

And once we're clear, once we have found a haven, somewhere that we feel safe... then perhaps we shall find each other again.

The remaining guard from the barracks prepares to drive the horse for us. The gladiators had despatched of any guards that tried to get in their way. Evidently, this one decided that helping us was a better option.

"Can we trust him?" I whisper.

"If he turns us over he'll have to pay for failing to protect the ludus. I think he was always on our side, anyway. He's barely more than a slave himself," Cassian mumbles, but I note the way he eyes the guard with caution.

Alba cries freely as Vitus tries to encourage her onto a horse. Her sweet face awash with the tears. She clutches me into an embrace and a sob escapes me. "I've seen the goodness inside you, Domina. I have belief in you. May the Gods be with you."

For once, I squash the voice inside – *don't show weakness, break them...*

I shut it down and let every bit of emotion pour from my face. I don't care that I'm crying too, or that I'm trembling. I bury my face into her neck and allow myself to feel her friendship, weeping that I have lost it before it could even begin.

"I will find you again, Alba... Gratitude." I let Cassian guide me away, into the waiting cart. We set off down the road and I glance back only once, just so I can see the devastation as our entire ludus burns to the ground.

52

LIVIA

My fingers trace along the tattoos on Cassian's arm. Black and dangerous. They give him an exotic edge, an extra dose of thrilling masculinity.

They will also draw a huge amount of unwanted attention. My touch finds the brand on his lower forearm. The mark of our ludus. One that identifies him as a slave, a gladiator, and now, as an escaped criminal.

"I will have it covered over," he says, following my gaze. "Or burned away." He shrugs, like either option is just fine.

We continue on in silence, and it isn't nearly long enough before it happens – our cart draws to a sudden halt, and rough male voices sound outside. I knew we'd encounter problems, but so soon...

My whole body stiffens. "This is just the beginning, Domina, but I will always protect you. I'm sworn to serve you, forever," Cassian whispers and shifts away, ready for confrontation.

"No." I take his hand. "You do not serve me. Not anymore. We stand equal. Together—"

The voices outside become louder, more agitated.

“What’s in the cart?” A gruff voice asks.

I peek through a gap in the wood and see the cohorts reaching for their weapons.

It takes mere seconds for Cassian to burst from the cart and end their lives.

I watch him in complete awe. This man will never be content with a life in hiding. He’s not made to cower, he’s made to fight. He might have escaped the ludus, the arena... but the battles are only just beginning.

He hops back into the cart and we continue down the road, leaving another three bodies in our wake.

“Livia,” he smiles, reaching out a hand to pull me into his safe embrace once more.

Livia.

He has never said that before.

I’ve always revelled in the way ‘Domina’ fell from his lips in an obedient mumble, but now, hearing him say my actual name...

“Livia,” he says again, testing it out on his tongue.

I pounce on him and delight in his touch, in his kiss – until he groans my name again and again and again.

53

CASSIAN

When she's eventually satiated from my kisses, Livia nestles down in the cart with her head in my lap and I stroke absently at her fiery hair.

Livia.

Words can barely even describe the feeling of speaking that name to her face without fear of reprisal. To groan her name and have her respond with love in her eyes.

The amount of times I wanted to ask her to run with me. Every time she appeared on the courtyard with a fresh bruise on her face, or with extra sorrow to her step – those days, I so badly wanted to scoop her up and run. But I didn't want her to have to experience poverty, not even for one day, let alone the rest of her life.

So I stayed. I buried those urges because at least there, at the ludus, I had a roof over my head and food in my belly, and she was safe.

Safe.

Wrong. You failed her. You let them abuse her too many times.

Never again.

I will never allow another man to touch her again. She belongs to me, and only me.

I can't remember when it changed. When I stopped hating her demands quite so much and started needing them. Somehow she worked her way under my armour and made me crave the very woman that I also wanted to kill.

It would have been so easy, on so many occasions. I could have put my hands around her throat and squeezed the life from her. Watched her face as she faded out of existence like so many others have done by my hands.

But looking at her now I see the real woman. Not the one living in her husband's shadow. Gone is the woman who was terrified by society's demands, who took pleasure in the suffering of others.

No, that's not true... I think she'll still enjoy a little suffering, but her targets have changed. Together we will fight for each other, and we will fight for them... for all the slaves, the gladiators, the abused women, the oppressed.

Perhaps we shall even bring Rome to its knees.

Because I was Death.

But together we are Hope.

ALSO BY NICOLA ROSE

Taste the Dark (Elwood Legacy 1)

One reckless girl and two vampire brothers – battling forces of love over lust, and light over dark...

Jess

I was 15 years old when our family home exploded in an atomic fashion, killing my parents. Thanks to convenient amnesia, I was left wondering what the hell happened, but without any doubt that I somehow caused it.

Cue years of flitting from one disaster to another, generally involving alcohol, drugs and bad boys. My new job on South Padre signified a turning point – time to sort myself out.

What I hadn't anticipated was the 6ft package of brooding, inked-up perfection who started stalking me. And don't even mention the equally hot brother crawling under my skin...

They radiate danger, it flows around them like a seductive spell; and danger is my favourite word.

Zac

I was doing a pretty good job at balancing on the fine line between light and dark, blurring the edges and living in the grey. But then dead vampires started piling up around me and the Bael gave me a ticking countdown to fix it.

Now she's arrived. Four seconds – the moment I saw her – that's how long it took to know that she'd simultaneously bring heaven and hell to my door. I don't even know what she is, but I know I crave her.

Falling for a human girl has left me teetering on the verge of collapse. This could be just the ammo my brother needs to nudge me over the edge and into oblivion.

Taste the Dark is a full-length paranormal romance, intended for adult audiences. Book one in the Elwood Legacy series.

ACKNOWLEDGMENTS

Thank you for reading Breaking the Gladiator.
I hope you enjoyed your time with Cassian! He's been stalking my thoughts for years now, so it feels wonderful to finally release him into the world!

Reviews are like gold to authors! Each one really does mean so much, even if it's only a few words! If you enjoyed reading, I hope you will consider leaving an honest rating on Amazon or Goodreads. Thank you!

ABOUT THE AUTHOR

Nicola Rose is from the UK, where she lives with her husband and two boys.

When she's not writing or reading, she can probably be found walking in the countryside, faffing in Photoshop, and playing boardgames (with varying degrees of aggression).

You may also find her obsessing over vampires and bad boys...

Find Nicola on Facebook, Instagram and Twitter.

www.nicolarose-author.com
Nicola@nicolarose-author.com

24743096R00082

Printed in Poland
by Amazon Fulfillment
Poland Sp. z o.o., Wrocław